Hunting Geese

Sarah Rau Peterson

Attention schools and businesses: for discounted copies
on large orders, please contact the publisher directly.

For information contact:
Unsolicited Press
Portland, Oregon
www.unsolicitedpress.com
orders@unsolicitedpress.com
619-354-8005

Cover Design: Kathryn Gerhardt
Editor: Kristen Marckmann

ISBN: 978-1-956692-19-8

Contents

Hunting Geese

Hunting Geese

HE'S PARKED ON THE RIVERBANK to get away from the wife, holding his thermos mug and staring out at the decoys. The sky has gone pink, and he's waiting for the geese to drop for their nightly visit. The shotgun's loaded but the safety's on and he can keep it on the seat next to him since Dog died. He sips his coffee-with-brandy, but it's lukewarm despite the thermos and the bitter taste gives him heartburn. The radio won't stop blaring talking head commentary about the upcoming presidential election—Jesus, it's still over a year away—and he wishes he could get a sports show, maybe some rock and roll out here instead. His hands ache from the cold, his old hands that have set hundreds, thousands of decoys into frozen riverbanks, lakeshores crusted with ice, waiting, waiting. He thinks of Freezeout Lake, so cold that winter—what, damn near forty years now—he remembers it was too cold to wait for the birds outside even though the first few were already scoping out his decoys. Scattered cars and pickups around the shorelines puffing clouds from the mufflers. He knew, too, that every one of those vehicles were tuned into the same AM station out of Calgary as he was, and nobody stopped listening even when the geese came down, and all at once the horns and flashing headlights, noise that all but drowned out the sound of the startled birds lifting off and out of range, but they all whooped and hollered, all the hunters like young boys, because they believed in miracles, yes they did, when the Ruskies lost that hockey game. The wife, a few years back he had told her about that cold night in '80, after they made that movie and everyone was talking about it again, and he teared up and then downright cried over how nobody pulled in any geese that night, but they were all brothers who emerged from warm vehicles to chant USA! USA! together into the frigid air. She wasn't really listening, he could tell, but he got downright pissed off when she told him she didn't remember it. Didn't remember it! Didn't remember the call? Al Michaels? Beating the freaking USSR, the Red Army guys? Her face was blank, and she'd said—she actually said—that she didn't follow football. He chuckles to himself, now. That had been a hell of a conversation. He warms his hands against the heater vent, rubs them together, arthritic knuckle against arthritic knuckle.

Oh, he still loves her, even though. He cuts her some slack, she's a good wife, and she eats the goose liver pate he makes with cut-up pickles even if she's never set a decoy, never field-dressed a bird in the cold and smelled the rusty scent of still-steaming blood, never even fired his shotgun. Even though she is clueless why he gets excited about Griz football, even though she laughs at the way he cries every time *Seven Bridges Road* comes on the oldies station. She teaches third grade, kids with bucked out teeth learning multiplication, and still cooks every night and does the laundry and even lets his old body climb on top of hers

8

once in a while. She can appreciate the sound of a thousand geese coming in to settle along the riverbank, she's told him so, the way she listens for it every night when she pulls in the driveway after school, her sensible shoes crunching the gravel, a cup of tea while grading papers. But damn.

She calls it anxiety when she gets worked up, and the therapist he sees at her request (always her request) calls it anxiety, but he calls it plain batshit. She complains about too many people in the grocery parking lot and that's why she didn't go in. The sound of the wind whistling around the eaves and she has to lie in bed, ears stuffed with cotton. An assembly at school that has made her nerves jangle like a tambourine. She says she's a sensitive person, but he can't put his finger on how she can wrangle twenty eight-year-olds all by herself, but she can't face the produce aisle. What he does understand is the sound of her voice when she's nagging him about leaving his tractor magazines on the couch, an empty coffee cup and dishes in the sink but not in the dishwasher, and don't even get her started on his habit of using a handkerchief (she calls it a snot rag) instead of a disposable tissue. The germs, she's worried about, says she gets enough of them in her classroom. He can't understand the sound of the heater cycling on so she can be comfortable, seventy-four degrees in the damn house, the electric bill climbing, her refusal to use the wood stove because it's dirty, when they have 500 acres of beetle-busted trees. Sometimes he feels like she's taken just about everything from him. He can't tell her that he uses handkerchiefs because his father did, because she only knew him as a drunk old bastard who did nothing but tell racist jokes first at the VFW and then in the VA. She didn't know Dad in his bronc days, back when he rodeo'd for so little in winnings, when Dad would come home with stitches in his chin or arm in a sling and a hospital bill, and he, just a youngster then, would get to rub down the bronc saddle with a special oil. How Mother worked nights in town emptying bedpans and wiping drool from toothless old mouths, just so Dad could rodeo and he always brought her something, usually beaded by the wives of the Indian riders. Mother's drive back home after work just in time to take his schoolboy self to the bus stop. He didn't tell the wife that Dad only started drinking hard after he broke his pelvis in a bad wreck with a bad bronc named Pearly Gates. How then, as a ten-year-old, he had to chop wood and haul square bales to the yearlings and the horses, how the work made him muscular and sad. How they had to sell everything, even the horses and the bronc saddle, the collection of beaded jewelry, and move to a rented house in town. The whiskey drinking like water. A neighbor man taking him on the banks of the Yellowstone for his first goose instead of Dad. The wife doesn't know all that because he hasn't told her in their fourteen years of marriage (a second for him, third for her), hasn't let her in to all the corners inside his heart, because if he starts telling, he might not stop and it's terrifying to have someone know all the parts of him. But *she* thinks he has, and she tells *him* everything, too much, like the time she got drunk as a high schooler and blew the starting five on the basketball team—she thinks these stories will bring them closer together.

Last night she ranted about his boots tracking mud—into the mudroom for Chrissakes, he'd said—and then it turned into the decoys in their mesh bags just where she wanted to park her car and gun oil smell in the kitchen, so he slept on the couch and stayed pretending to be asleep until she left for school. Before she got home he loaded his pickup bed with the decoys and the shotgun he plans to give his own son for a gift when he finally comes clean about his relationship with his "roommate." Oh, he knows all right what that means. He isn't stupid even if he was brought up traditional—hell, his own parents had had twin beds—but he is mad that the son tries to disguise it, doesn't have enough faith in his old man to tell him the truth. And God, but when he tries to talk to the wife about it, she has all kinds of things to say to prove she's okay with it but still uses words like "the gays" and once, "those people," which to him grated like a bad wheel but he didn't say boo to her because she's not the boy's mother. Now, he lights a cigarette, a habit he hides from her and only does when he's well away from the house. Blows the smoke through the window he's rolled open, revs the engine a bit to keep the heater chugging warmth. He punches the button to silence the radio, so all he hears is the crackle of the icy river and his own breath.

And the girl, he thinks, his daughter, with her high Slavic cheekbones and eyes like a cat from her mother's mother, and he just knew as she had grown older and more beautiful that people questioned her paternity, wondered if that was the secret to implode that marriage and left him with not much more than a pickup full of decoys and his three-legged dog named Dog. Smart and sassy since the day she was born, that one. She never called him Daddy, must have heard everyone else call him Harv, and so she did from the time she could talk.

She always went her own way, and he was proud of her when she up and moved to Texas to work at a horse ranch. He still thought of her sometimes as a girl who played ponies while riding a broomstick through the kitchen, and not as the teenager busted for smoking marijuana and then let off with only probation when the drug test also revealed a pregnancy, because he could never reconcile the two girls in his mind. He blamed himself for the divorce that happened when she was a child, thought she wouldn't have turned out the way she did, and he blamed himself after the arrest and the announcement and told her out of pure anger that he would remove the guy's balls and hang them from his rearview because damn it, didn't she know better and why was she so stupid. And then she called him a week later and told him not to worry because it was done now, and her voice was flat and she said she'd enrolled in an equine studies program at the JC for early admission while she finished high school, and he'd immediately regretted his words and his anger and his inability to see the girl inside.

He stubs out his cigarette on the pocked dashboard and pockets the butt, reminds himself to get rid of it before laundry day. Sips at the coffee and shudders at its taste and at the emotion building from thinking about his children, the way it makes his heart ache and the tears fall from his eyes, and he thinks of his father, how he would laugh at the tears, how he always laughed and called him a bawl baby, a milk-sucking calf. He thinks of his wife, saying she's sensitive. But it's only here that he can let it out, when the weak sun leaves the cottonwoods in shadows on the east-flowing river, it's here that he can think about the mistakes he's made with his children and both of his marriages, can think about Dog, who finally died in his sleep at fifteen years old, the three legs twitching a final gallop in the night and lying cold on the floor when he went to feed him that morning. The tears roll down the lines in his face and catch in his moustache, and he can't believe he's still crying about that dog, even though it's been a goddamn year, but he remembers Dog as a pup, when his daughter was still a child and screamed every night in her sleep, and he'd went to the pound for a kitten, something to keep her company and instead found this sad little creature, all black and white fluff and smiling border collie face, and the lady there had said that they'd gotten rid of the rest of the litter, even the mother, but nobody wanted a dog born with only three legs, and that had touched his heart enough to pay the adoption fee, sign the paper that promised a neuter, and brought the dog home to the house where his marriage was already flailing, a kite loosed on the wind. It was enough trying to house-break a three-legged dog, enough on top of that wife who was sick and tired of him always working in the field, always hunting in his spare hours, and she didn't realize the Fed job that required him to be in the field put money in their bank account and gave health insurance to the family, that the hunting put good deer on the table, a goose for the holidays, jerky for an after-school snack. It never was enough for her, and it was almost a relief when it was over, but nearly every day since then (even now, all these years later), the guilt stabs him in the gut, gives him diarrhea in the middle of the night, when he thinks that if he'd only stuck it out that the kids wouldn't have moved on and out, that maybe his son would be in the pickup with him in the cold, sticking goose deeks into the frozen dirt, instead of clear to Missoula at the big outdoors store where he worked, or the daughter would still be interested in cleaning the purplish gizzard to find the grit inside, something that still amazes him, the way a bird's body works.

God, but the things he finds peace in, now. The bench seat of the pickup still sheds fine white hair from Dog, and he's glad to have saved that pup from the pound and the inevitable cold injection to stop his heart, his body tossed in the incinerator with the others, the worthless, the old and sick. The way the cold bites at him in his fingerless gloves, makes his skin crack and bleed every time he sets the deeks; even that gives him peace, the routine of it a ritual. The way the river sounds when he's the only one to hear it. The leafless cottonwoods that line the riverbank, limbs like his own old fingers grasping at the sky. The winter is enough to send him weeping into his handkerchief, the thick hair on his horses beautiful and life-affirming, the sound of their hooves on a crust of snow. The spring, the buds on the trees, the smell of earthworms and dirt and brand new calves still covered in birth fluid. The summer heat, alfalfa cut, dried, and baled before a storm hits, sweaty armpits from the un-air-conditioned hay truck, the taste of a cold beer like gold. The brilliance of fall, leaves drying and dying, a bonfire in the slash pile where he watches from a nearby stump, brandy in his coffee. He can cry just thinking about all of these things he does, he sees and smells, over the course of the seasons, and it almost makes him ashamed, these emotions.

His father never got worked up about the seasons, the earth and its land, the river. His father never cried, not when he returned home with a broken body, not when he lost himself trying to find the bottom of a whiskey bottle, not when he was widowed and spent his days at the VFW from open to close. Not even in his last years in the VA when he stared right in the face of his mortality; no, he was an ornery old coot, pinching the nurses' asses and spitting phlegm into a Coke can. Telling jokes about Mexicans and Indians, about their food and their bodies and their drunkenness, jokes that everybody laughed at, politely, meeting knowing glances above his eye level there in the bed. He sat in his own waste because his legs were gone by that point, because he was too stubborn, too drunk to take care of himself and just see a doctor already, and the infection that set in his knee, infectious arthritis, they'd said, was just too dangerous to treat with antibiotics alone, especially since he kept drinking; they'd had to mete out

15

shots of whiskey throughout his amputation and recovery so he wouldn't die from the shock of withdrawal.

No, the crying came from a place deep inside his body, and he pictured (although he knew anatomy) his heart connected directly to the thought center of his brain with a cord like those old curly telephone wires, that made his chest squeeze and his eyes water with most any thought, the damn trees for Chrissakes, the way the sun sets into pink and orange and seven shades of blue, the sound of the geese he can hear for miles, and the noise they make, the sheer number of them, it's like a train landing there on the bank among his decoys, and he blows his nose into his handkerchief and then stuffs it into the pocket of his woolen vest, swipes at his eyes with his rough fingertips. He's parked behind a dense copse of juniper, and if he can get out without much movement or noise, he's pretty sure he can knock a few out, he doesn't need many, from right where he's standing.

He sighs, removes the key from the ignition and opens the pickup door, leaves it open as he shoulders his shotgun. It's time to kill some birds.

Chickens

SOMETHING IS EATING MY CHICKENS. Levi has noticed a fox den, stinking on the hillside, red tufts of fur matted into the brush, but I can't believe my dogs would let a fox get so close to the house. It could be a raccoon, rummaging and scavenging up from the mucky old corrals down below the house, but the garbage is intact, and again, the dogs. The hens are two and three years old and so plump I can't imagine a hawk or an eagle passing through would get one, although I won't rule it out. It's a night hunter for certain, because every morning when I get up, feed the worthless dogs, and head to the hen house for eggs, I'm greeted with another patch of feathers, far too much for a simple spring molting, and the hens are squirrely on their eggs, pecking at my hands, and the empty nesting boxes stare at me. Goldie, Snowflake, Penny, Brownie . . . they are gone.

I wasn't raised to be any sort of a farm girl, certainly not one Levi's great-grandmother, who homesteaded just up the draw, would recognize, but I enjoy pretending. Her house was next to an alkali spring below a sloping, sage-brushed hill, the spring so mineral-rich that the great-grandfather wouldn't let his horses drink from it, but you can bet it was good enough for cooking and washing and drinking, even if it tasted like blood from the iron deposits (it does, I've tasted it). And our house, a modular thing that came in two halves on the backs of two semis—she'd certainly have something to say about that. Hers was rough cut pine boards set upon a stone foundation that the great-grandfather built himself, although all that still stands is a crooked stone outline nearly overcome with cheatgrass. But I have chickens, because I think they are funny to watch peck around the yard and it's nice to have fresh eggs. Levi hates them because they like to roost on his tractors and his hay truck, and chickens are not known for being discriminating or polite poopers. But he helped me build a coop out of a shipping crate and some old tin, and now the coop sits unprotected from a night stalker right next to the wood shed on the side of the house.

Levi's great-grandmother surely had an entire yard full of hens in her time, eggs with which to bake and to sell in town along with cream from the milk cow; I'm pretty sure my great-grandmother was the kind of town folk who would have purchased those eggs and cream, cringing at the feathers and poop clinging to the shells. To learn some of the things I think I should know, I subscribe to the kinds of dippy magazines that taught me how to raise backyard hens and create tablecloths and matching triangular banners from vintage sheets.

It's the combination of my stubbornness and wannabe hippie ways that has prevented the building of a long run for the hens, protected from the dogs and other beasts that slink around the ranch. The best eggs! Free range! The magazine headlines shout at me about the natural ways to raise hens. I'm not stuck on the humanity of it, though; ranch life isn't for the faint-hearted when it comes to animal treatment. I've held a cat in the sleeve of an old coat while Levi castrated it with an X-Acto knife, the cat pissed off and yowling but no worse for the wear when all was cut and done. I feed my dogs expensive food but they sleep outside on all but the absolute coldest days of winter; they don't get much more than a spay (at the vet, at least) and an annual rabies shot. No, it's not necessarily that I want my eggs to come from happy, uncontained chickens; I'd just like my eggs to come from chickens that aren't dying one at a time, disappearing in the night in a cloud of feathers and not a beak or foot or drop of blood left.

I've Googled it, and I spread a thick layer of cheap flour (not the Wheat Montana stuff I buy for baking, but the kind that is so fine, it sifts through the inexpensive paper wrapping while still in my cart at the grocery store) all around the hen house, right at dusk, after the hens have found their own way back to their house, water pans full and food buckets topped off. I toss it right out of the bag as I walk backwards, the slight breeze coating my body with a dusting so I look like a ghost in the fading light. I brush off my hands on my pants, and Levi laughs at the handprints I've left on my backside, places his own calloused hands in the prints, squeezes. I swat him away and ask him what kind of predatory footprints I might expect to see in the flour in the morning.

"Cat . . . coon . . . Big Foot," he says with a straight face. I frown. This is serious to me. I've named the hens, hauled home fifty-pound sacks of feed, twenty-pound blocks of grain they can peck, gallons of water from the pump. I've collected worms from the garden and taken pictures of the chickens fighting and pecking each other for the juiciest one. I've spread their waste-filled straw on the garden and mulched it into the dirt. I've placed their dirty eggs in a basket, not washing them until ready to use. I feel like a farm girl for sure with my hens.

"Something is getting them," I tell him. "I need to find out what."

"I know," he sighs. "But you can't expect a long lifetime out here if you don't keep them penned up." He's right, I know. "That reminds me," he continues, squeezing my butt again, "One of them crapped all over the bale feeder."

I spin away from him, start to scrub my hands in the sink. "I'll clean it tomorrow."

"I'm feeding at eight," he reminds me, as if I could forget his daily routine of loading bales of hay out for the cows until the weather warms and the grass greens up. As if I could forget scrubbing chicken poop off the rack every morning before he feeds, silently cursing both him—park somewhere else—and them—roost somewhere else—while dissolving the white clumps with vinegar.

"I said I'll do it," I snap.

We dish up our dinners and go our separate ways, him to the couch in front of the TV, where he alternately watches Fox News, ESPN, and the National Geographic

Channel, none of them long enough to glean any information. I sit at the counter in front of my computer, a fork in one hand, the other pecking a letter at a time into Google—fox-proofing a hen house, how to get rid of raccoons. I get a lot of results that pander to the "everyone has a right to eat and live, especially when you're on their territory" folks, and I close the laptop.

After dinner, dishes rinsed and dishwasher humming, Levi heads to the shower and I step out onto the deck for my nightly cigarette. The chill on the false wooden decking seeps through my slippers. It's full dark now, but the moon is nearly full, and it shines a dusky glow onto the pastures of dead grass, makes the trees into shadows. When it is full, you almost don't need headlights, and any nighttime activity on the open pasture is a dangerous venture. I can sometimes hear the barn owl that lurks high up in the grove of cottonwoods along the reservoir, but except for a breeze whispering through the trees, it's quiet tonight. I can see just a corner of the flour floor I've poured around the henhouse from where I stand, if I lean my elbows onto the deck rail. Even by the light of the almost-moon, I can tell nothing has left a single footprint. The remaining hens are making their night noises, some clucking and clicking as they settle down for the night in the nest boxes I've filled with straw and pine shavings, and one raucous flapping of feathers and a quick squawk from Gladys, the only golden one left, Gladys who always makes a big show. I think that whatever is getting to the hens certainly has their work cut out for them with her.

The flash of movement catches my eye, there beyond the wire fence line. I squint, and the moonlight is just bright enough. I see her. I know, instinctively somehow, that it's a female. She senses me, I think, maybe catches the scent of my still-unlit cigarette, and she stops. I can just see her tail, bushy and erect, her alert ears and the way her coat fades into white under her chin. She's smaller than I imagined, not much bigger than a good-sized tomcat. She's still, and she looks right at me. I can feel her liquid eyes moving over my still form above her, perched on the deck. There's still a bit of rustling from the hen house and her ears flick toward the sound. Her tail twitches softly, just the very tip of it moving, a darker shadow in the darkish night. I can smell her, not as well as she must smell me; she's slightly skunky, but different, maybe an underlayer of rotten meat. It's the same smell Levi has talked about around the den, musky he said, all animal. I stay perfectly still, watching. She ventures a step forward, all four paws shifting softly, and stops, never moving her eyes from me. I can make out the low hang of her belly; Levi says the reason she's denned up is to raise kits. I know it's her now, the one who is making nighttime visits to haul off my hens, one at a time.

We watch each other. Gladys has settled and there is no more noise from the hens. There's the moon, the tree shadows. Me. A mother fox. From somewhere in the back of my brain I remember that she's called a vixen. A vixen, just over the fence from my yard, and yet the dogs have no clue. I think to shout, to call to them, to wave my arms, chase her away, but she sits down, tail swishing against the dead grass, still alert. I think of how her coat must look in daytime, or against the snow. I think of Levi and his buddies, rifles, ammo, and a case of beer, readying for a coyote hunt, where a nice one with a light-colored but winter-heavy pelt will bring forty bucks, a little less for a rusty red fox slung over a tailgate, fur buyers handing out greasy twenties from a roll, pickups lined up in the back alley of a bar, full of drunk hunters and dead furbearers. Varmints, the old timers will shout from barstools. Kill 'em all. But then what, I think, staring at her. Then we have too many mice and packrats and cottontails and voles and prairie dogs and nothing left to get them except the big birds and the kids with .22s.

The fox yawns. Is she bored with me already? We've only just met. I've caught you almost in the act. You should run away before I get Levi and his rifle. All this to myself, but I know she'll be gone by then, probably with Gladys's golden feathers dripping from her jaw.

But then I remember. A hungry and howling baby in the crib, milk dripping from my swollen breasts and through my shirt as I mumble an excuse to get off the phone. That baby, older, screeching in the seat of the grocery cart because I can't open the can of dissolvable baby puffs (unpaid for, still) fast enough. Screaming for a sippy cup of milk. Yowling, demanding, big crocodile tears for anything to be put into that constantly open maw of a mouth, until that baby grew up, eating a box of cereal and a gallon of milk in a mixing bowl before baseball practice.

Until that open maw moved out and on and I rejoiced, yes I did, because my grocery bill went down the two hundred dollars that I spent every single month for over eighteen years to feed him—just him— until I fell into bed many nights, exhausted and unshowered and crying real tears at the expense and effort it took to keep another human alive for just one more day. It was damn hard, damn expensive. I remember the effort, the deep-seeded need a mother has to see her child with a full belly, drifting sated and quiet into sleep, and the peace and the fulfillment of raising a baby into toddlerhood, into school, into adulthood.

I get it, I say in my head to the fox. The vixen. I stand straight up and she rises to her feet.

"You win," I tell her, aloud. Her ears twitch, her tail drops low. I snap the unlit cigarette in half and toss the pieces into the yard. "I guess I'll just buy the damn eggs." And I enter the house, leave her to get on with it.

The Needing Place

SATURDAY, MY PHONE BEEPED, REMINDED me to visit Dad—yes, I needed a reminder. I filled my travel mug with coffee, pulled on my chore boots, and drove out to the ranch. I found him in the corral up to his ankles in mud and cow shit with a gate balanced on one knee as he tried to lift the other end onto a bolt.

"Damn heifers busted through," he said by way of greeting. He had an unlit cigarette clenched between his teeth. I lifted the green metal pipe off his knee and told him it was too heavy for him to do himself.

"Call me for help, Dad. You shouldn't be doing this yourself."

"I can do it," he growled, but the gate slipped easily onto the bolt with my help. He latched it with a chain around the railroad tie brace.

"Where'd the heifers go?" I asked.

"Ran off to section nine," he said with a final rap to the bolt with his mallet. My ears rang.

Section nine, full of pine trees. Dad'd preg-tested only a month ago, gotten rid of his dries. It was freezing at night, but softly, melting into mud in the morning; he wasn't feeding bales yet even though I had told him to start. The heifers with their first calves on board needed the extra

25

nutrition, and they'd sure enough searched it out. Problem was, pine needles send cows into abortive spasms, causing premature and nonliving birth.

I hadn't lived on the ranch since eighteen when I left for college in Missoula, and from there to Helena. I moved back after Mom died, bought a historic-registered Victorian on Main Street, sent one kid on an academic scholarship to the University of Montana and the other to Montana State, did my textbook editing job in the third story office of my home, helped Dad when I could or wanted to. My half-brother John—Mom's son from before—has been out of the picture since the time Dad called him a "homo" for teaching band at the high school. Dad didn't call me; I called him. I picked him up—a forty-four mile round trip—to host holidays at my house, and then brought him home after he'd drank too much whiskey and had eaten and sat sullenly in the corner recliner. He was short when the boys tried to talk to him. Clipped and gruff when my husband asked about the ranch. I had failed him, I knew. Failed him first by being born a girl, failed him by going to 'that hippie school,' when the local community college was good enough, nearly too good for him because 'you don't need a damn piece of paper to fix fence,' but at least they had a rodeo team where I could have found a husband. Failed him by marrying Gary, a suit-and-tie banker from Kalispell who hadn't ever pulled a calf and sewn up a prolapsed uterus in the middle of the night. I had failed him, and he was an old bastard. My dad.

"I'll go get them," I said, already walking to his beat-up four-wheeler.

"No," Dad said. He headed toward the house, boots sucking mud with every step. "I don't need your help."

Bitty, his old red heeler, raised her head from her den under the porch, woofed at us, and settled back down. I could smell her from three feet away, the cancer that was eating her from the inside out. Dad stomped into the house; I saw him stare at me from the kitchen window, the curtain Mom had sewn from an old sheet hiding and revealing, hiding and revealing half his face with his breath. I guess he decided I could do it.

I followed the cow tracks in the gumbo, the fresh green shit piles, up to section nine. The four-wheeler whined and hurt my instep when I shifted with the foot lever, bumped over ruts with its worn-out shocks. The hand grips were worn down to metal in places. I found the heifers, about twenty or so, underneath a stand of ponderosa. A few of them were neck-stretched into the lowest branches.

"Get! Get!" I yelled, gunned the engine to startle them. "Yah! Hey hey! Get moving!" I swerved around them, slipping a bit in the mud. The heifers bucked and kicked but moved as one toward the corrals, back down the hill, hooves sucking gumbo and ear tags bobbing with their heads. I rode around back of them.

"Shit," I swore. Several of the heifers had red strands of placenta hanging out under their tails, fluids dripping. I gunned at them another time to keep them running down the hill and drove to where they had been standing underneath the pines. Sure enough.

The cauls had been licked away from them, the birth instinct strong even in heifers, even when they slough a lifeless form. Gelatinous hooves, white and gooey, eyes just a dark bulge under the surface of slick pink skin.

"Damn it," I said over the fetuses. There were seven. Seven goddamn aborted calves. I looked up; turkey vultures hulked in the naked trees.

"Get!" I yelled and flapped my arms, but they just stared at me from their red heads, waiting to gorge.

I drove down to the corral where the heifers had clustered around the gate. I shooed them away, opened it, chased them through, looped the chain to close it. The windbreak along the north side of the corral had rotted down and there was at least one hole big enough for the heifers to just walk right out. I found a couple of rusted barrels in the old grain shed and rolled them down, placed them upright in front of the hole. It wouldn't hold a rangy heifer intent on busting out, but it might deter her for an hour or so. A barrel the size of Custer County wouldn't repair all the holes worn into this ranch, I thought as I drove back to the house. I was again greeted by the stink and woof of Bitty from under the porch.

"Dad?" I called as I let myself in. I took off my boots in the mudroom but soon noticed I shouldn't have bothered. Muddy footprints led the way into the kitchen, to the fridge, down the carpet to the bathroom, to the kitchen table . . . Dad's trails looked like a crazy dance routine and smelled like the corrals. The table was covered with copies of the Farm and Ranch Weekly newspaper. Coffee cups half full. Plates with egg yolks petrifying. Oily parts from some machine. There was an overwhelming smell of mice on top of everything.

"Dad?" I called again as I poured the coffees down the sink, turned on water over the plates. The faucet was crusted with lime deposits and the water only came out in jerks and spurts and smelled metallic.

"Quit yer yellin'," Dad said as he emerged from the bathroom. He was still buttoning his pants, pulling his suspenders over his shoulders.

"I got the heifers in, but seven of them sloughed their calves." Dad was bent over the woodstove, shoving pieces in with his foot and the poker and didn't hear me. He closed the door and slammed down the rod that worked the damper.

"What you say?" He straightened up with a grimace and I heard his back crack and pop even from across the room. Vietnam followed by fifteen years breaking rough stock for the Five Brands Rodeo Company meant seven different back surgeries and, now, a yearly epidural in his lumbar spine. I remember being a small kid and rubbing Icy Hot on his back at night, avoiding the blue lumps of shrapnel working their way to the surface near his shoulder. It almost embarrasses me as an adult to know his back so intimately, the scars that run from his neck to the middle, then from the middle to his hip. I remember a constellation of moles that I would connect with my fingertips. He used to call the scars his roadmaps. I'd go to sleep with my hands burning and smelling of menthol, careful not to touch my eyes. I haven't seen him without a shirt in decades, and I wonder about the lumps of shrapnel.

"I said that I got the heifers back to the corral. They could use another bale down there." I paused. "A few of them aborted."

Dad looked out the filmy window above the sink. It was starting to sleet. "Goddamn pine needles. Stupid bitch heifers." I couldn't tell if he was talking to me or himself. He poured himself a cup of coffee from the pot on the stove; his old-fashioned way of making coffee was the reason I had brought my own. His mug was a cheap-looking freebie from the John Deere dealership. I'd probably find the one with the boys' school pictures inserted behind plastic stuffed on the top shelf, yellowing and unused.

"You want me to do anything?" I asked him, knowing his answer. "I could grab your prescriptions from town and bring them back out with a lasagna or something."

"I can do that my damn self. I gotta worry about them heifers right now. Get 'em to the winter pasture before they all shit out dead calves. You better get back to your town now." And there it was. My town. No matter that he and Mom used to eat at the Hole in the Wall once a month, treat themselves to a prime rib and a couple of whiskey ditches. Bloody Marys at the Bison Bar during the Bucking Horse Sale parade every May, Irish coffee there during the February bull sale. He probably hadn't been anywhere other than the John Deere dealership and the feed store in years. The grocery store for a cheap can of coffee, some frozen meals, paid for with a check pre-filled in his crabbed cursive because he couldn't be inside the store for more than a few minutes without the fluorescent lights bothering him.

He didn't need me.

She Would Have

THE CORNER POSTS OF THE GATE were inward-leaning, and holes the size of his fist were forming and caving around the bases. He thought of the pile of railroad ties he'd purchased at the auction sale last year—for the sole purpose of replacing these very posts—eight bucks a piece, now just rotting into a pile and poisoning his dirt with creosote.

"Maybe if John was worth a good God damn," he muttered. He couldn't fathom his son who wasn't even *his* son, the boy who'd come with Esme as a package deal and now long-wounded from a forgotten argument, principal or some such in the high school, breaking up fights between knucklehead punks, instead of doing something that mattered, working with his hands instead of his mouth. They hadn't spoken in eleven or so years.

He pulled his cattle stick from behind the pickup seat and poked at the bucket of fencing tools that had slid to the middle of the pickup bed until he could reach it.

"Maybe if them boys weren't up to chasin' tail and wastin' money at school, they'd a' helped me put in them ties." His grandsons, one at the University of Montana, the younger one at Montana State, the entire damn family making a big deal about it.

He grabbed the bucket and heaved it to the ground with a grunt that startled a magpie, sent it squawking and flapping its long tail to the next pile of death. The weak afternoon light caused shadows on the rutted ground that he didn't see. The morning's sleet had stopped, but the clouds hung low and the air had a damp chill that burned his ears. He'd forgotten his cap.

He didn't bother to attach the sissified gate latch the kid at the hardware store sold him; just pulled and squeezed the gate post until it slipped under the oft-repaired wire to hold it shut. He hooked the broken wire into the stretcher, barbs catching on his calloused hands and drawing seeps of blood that he didn't feel. With aching knuckles he stretched the wire to a semblance of tightness and tapped a new staple to the post to hold the slack. He missed the staple more than he hit it, and chunks of rotting wood chipped off with each miss. He leaned his body into the brace post and pushed, kicked some sticky clods of mud down into the hole. The kicking hurt his toes in his muck boots and his shoulder was aching where he leaned into the gate post. Still it listed.

Fuck it. He tossed the wire stretcher onto the bed of the pickup. Cold air seeped into the hole in his coat, leached into the worn flannel shirt underneath. His hands ached, his back ached. He still had to move the heifers.

Once, he couldn't think to when, it seemed so long ago, he didn't ache and he followed the life cycle of his

34

land; he was just the messenger for the work that nature dictated. Spring, calves born, tagged, branded. Summer, hay cutting and baling and hauling, or in a drought, more years than not, saving weather reports from the newspaper and poring over them, looking for a pattern, for that front that might bring some moisture. Turn out the bulls. Bring in the bulls. Contract calves for sale. Fall, cow work: preg-testing, pre-conditioning vaccines for the calves; finally, the paycheck. Winter, pay the bills, unroll bales every day in the snow, pickax ice from the water tanks. Plow snow. Chop firewood. Look for that first crocus poking through the snow, for that first bulging bag of amniotic fluid under a cow's tail to signify the return of spring, the starting again.

That circle was caving in on itself, now.

He didn't know the exact moment he got old. When Catherine graduated college, he didn't even go. It was May and he was already late spraying the east section against the goddamn weevils. When she got married to that banker, he took three days off for the winter ceremony, traveled to Red Lodge and bitched the whole damn time about the expense and the cold and the fact that he had to rely on the eighteen-year-old kid from a neighboring ranch to feed the cows. He spent a lot of time in the hotel lobby's phone bank, calling the long distance charge number on the back of his credit card to check in with that kid. He took home a burning in his gut that has never gone. Her twins were born, boys, thank the damn lord, and he saw them a total of two times before they were in school. Esme, now, she stayed with Catherine for a whole month after their birth, and then drove clear to Helena to visit at least once a month. She was even there for the birth; she called in happy tears with the news, a bit premature but "everyone is fine, they're fine, we're all fine," it reminded him of Number 81, a Hereford cross who, in the middle of a late-February snowstorm, shat out twin premature calves. He'd hauled them home on the bench seat of his pickup, heater on high, and slapped them in the bathtub under a warm tap. Catherine was a kid, probably eight, pig-tailed anyway; she watched from the doorway. Those early twin calves died right there in his tub while his kid watched, nothing and everything he could have done. She'd cried. When her babies were born, that's what he pictured, her crying at dead calves. Big-eyed, little girl tears. Esme didn't call home for a week when he told her that. He couldn't even remember where John was when those calves died.

Hell, obituaries in the paper had folks he knew, or at least knew of. Esme used to attend a book group with a few women in various stages of decay, but he figured they just bitched about their husbands and drank wine and showed pictures of grandchildren. Esme wasn't old in the way he saw the other ladies. She smelled like lemon soap, not like funeral flowers. She didn't have that turkey thing under her jaw; she wore jeans and boiled-wool clogs like some sort of hippie, with her braid, gone gray and her being too practical to color it, down the middle of her back.

And then she died. Just keeled over in the garden, she fell to the earth next to the heavy tomato plants, with Bitty by her side until he came home from stacking hay bales. She looked like she had just lay down to take in the smell of the ripening fruits, something she always loved, but Bitty barked and barked and he knew. He had to call John, break his heart, and he had to call Catherine in Helena and break hers too. And he had to do all of the things one does in those circumstances. Those boys of Catherine's wore matching suits to the church, and with their complex basketball shoes and fresh haircuts he didn't even *know* them, still didn't know them even though Catherine had moved them all back, even that prim husband of hers, after Esme. John in a shiny suit, shaking hands with his clean fingernails. Then the casseroles came, and the cards, but then those dropped off after a while and he was just another coot trying to scrape together his ranch and his life. Twelve years ago. He can grow zucchini if he feels like it, but not tomatoes. Never tomatoes. *Now* he's old.

The pickup was slow to start—the oil change overdue by months and miles—and the clutch was tricky and the brake pedal loose, and he found a mouse nest in the jockey box when he rummaged for the pint he kept rat-holed inside. He'd never kept a pint hidden anywhere when Esme was alive, never had to feel that first burn. He took a swig and felt the warmth of the whiskey as it moved through his body. He knew it, with those damn blood thinners his doctor made him take, could kill him—BAM—and he was sure nobody would find him until long after the coyotes did.

He remembered the day they bought the pickup—the damp, chill air at the outside spring auction, a Styrofoam cup of bitter coffee in one hand, the numbered buyer's card in the other. Esme had gone to rifle through the table full of unnecessary trinkets (dust-collectors like music boxes and table-top picture frames) while he was left alone in the dirt parking lot of the auction yard. The pickup came after a Case front-loader tractor that went for a thousand dollars more than it was worth. The truck was dirty and some greaseball kid had written "cocksucker" in the dust on the tailgate, it had two low tires that made it stand lopsided, and the doors were locked so he couldn't get inside. The auctioneer said it had close to two hundred thousand miles on it, but was good for more. He didn't care; he just needed a new truck that would withstand the rutted ranch roads after Esme complained about the broken heater on the old one. He was the only bidder and thought that everyone else knew something he didn't about that truck, but when the sale was over, the auctioneer filled up the low tires and accepted his rumpled, damp check. When he unlocked the doors, the interior smelled like old beer and mice. A damn gallon of that fancy spray stuff wouldn't get the smell out, he'd thought. Esme hadn't bid on any of the trinkets.

But now he had to get the heifers out of the corral. Where he'd left them for two days because his back ached so bad he hadn't the will to drive that last group of 'em to the winter pasture, especially now that Bitty slept under the porch and stank of the cancer that was dissolving her guts and was no good help. He was sure he hadn't shut the corral gate tight enough—damn chain latch burned his hands with cold—and couldn't remember if he'd written down the ear tag numbers so he'd be able add them to his pocket-sized record book. Esme would have. He took another drink. And another. Drove home.

Wednesday's Child

I DID EVERYTHING RIGHT. I breastfed. I volunteered in the classroom, even if it meant using a half-day of vacation time. I sent raisins and carrots instead of cupcakes for Valentine's parties. I read to her. I listened while she read to me. I drove her to dance lessons, to piano lessons, to birthday parties. I sat in too-small chairs at parent-teacher conferences and nodded at her teachers, thanked them for meeting with me after work. I always called the school by 8:30 when she was sick, after I called my boss. But Dan left as she was due to start seventh grade, citing his need to get back to the mountains, and I wanted to stay where she was growing up; yes, it really was that easy. I bought her a cell phone so she could call me when she walked home from school; she insisted she was the very last of her friends to have a phone. She was probably right. She declared Facebook for "losers and nerds" and I agreed to Instagram, but only if she added me as a friend (I had to quickly learn all the terminology, the hashtags, the double-taps). She signed up for cheerleading. I signed her up for counseling to talk about the divorce. Her grades fell, then rose again. The counselor told me she was doing great and was well-adjusted. She had friends, good girls who played sports and instruments. They had sleepovers and texted boys. I got an app that let me know what she was downloading. As she got older, she retreated into her bedroom, into fashion magazines and her unexplainable music (at least with earbuds), and I, who had once smuggled a Metallica tape into my parents' Catholic home and rolled the skirt of my uniform whenever the nuns weren't looking, thought it was all normal. It probably was.

I had a good job at the bank, didn't work past five and had all the holidays and weekends off. We went to movies together sometimes, shared popcorn and the big diet soda. We went to the beauty college and had cheap pedicures. She visited Dan in the summer, by train up to Whitefish, and she texted me pictures of her young body in a bikini that I didn't buy her, pictures of her and Dan in goofy fishing hats and vests covered with lures. She came home tan with sunny streaks in her hair, an appreciation for swimming in the frigid waters of Flathead Lake. She felt refreshed, she said. I knew from Instagram she had met a boy—pictures of them taken at arms' length on the dock, licking the same ice cream cone. I took group sessions at the church from the new progressive priest about single-parenting the millennials. I learned to say "selfie" even though it made me feel ridiculous. I didn't ask her about the boy.

And so it went through high school. Friends came and went as they do. Boys, too, nice guys who started on the football team, played baseball or worked for the city in the summer. Boys who shook my hand. I took her to the doctor and waited without judgment when she wanted birth control pills for her heavy period—I was certain that wasn't the reason, but I let it slide no matter how hard it was to bite my tongue against my own upbringing. We didn't argue much, didn't disagree over curfew or grades or really anything until we started talking college. I wanted her to stay at home, take a couple years at Miles Community College until she figured out what she wanted to do. "Nobody has careers anymore, Mom," she whined. "It doesn't really matter." But it did matter, to me. I wanted more for her than an office job, something with substance. Something she felt passionate about, and I didn't want to spend money at a larger school until she figured it out. There were too many distractions, too many courses and classes and friends and boys and new experiences to just wing it.

I hadn't gone to college. I learned typing (on actual typewriters!) in high school, and I started as a teller at the bank the day after I graduated. It wasn't a huge deal. I figured I'd marry a local boy, a hardworking boy from a ranch or with an auto-repair business in the family, because that was what my mother wanted for me, what I was expected to do even toward the end of the millennium. Work for a bit until "he" comes along. I met Dan instead when I had just turned nineteen. He was working with the Corps of Engineers to add dirt to the river's dike in case the great flood came. He had long golden hair tied in a ponytail, and he took communion at the Saturday night service just like we did. I could have done worse in my parents' eyes, but I could have done a lot better. He was a "nice boy," they said, even though he had long hair, wore holey jeans and had a roach clip (not that they knew what that was) dangling from the rear view of his company truck. He had coffee with the priest and mowed the lawn outside the rectory. I had to wear skirts and nylons at the bank, sweaters that buttoned to the collarbone even though it was the 90s. I lived at home until he proposed, fresh with a job at the fisheries station and a rented home on the north side of town. Erika was born an exact nine months after our big, solemn wedding (complete with Mass!), on the bright but cold Wednesday before Easter, and you can bet there were a lot of people counting on their fingers. I still wasn't old enough to drink.

"I like the mountains," she'd said, when I asked her about college. It was her father's ski trips to Big Mountain, pack trips into the Bob Marshall with a team of mules and horses and a big wall tent, summers in a cabin on Flathead that she remembered.

"But you can transfer," I argued. "Bozeman and Missoula both will take an Associate Degree, no questions. You'll jump right in to whatever program you want."

"But I won't. KNOW. ANYBODY. THEN," she shouted at me, slammed the door into her bedroom, only to retreat a moment later without making eye contact to pick up the pink-cased phone she left on the table.

Dan and I didn't communicate that often, mostly just to arrange pick-up and drop off for Erika's visits. I mailed him photocopies of her report cards because even though he, as her father, could access the school's online parent portal, he didn't have a computer and still used a flip phone. Our arrangement was made easier by the fact that he didn't dispute anything. He didn't want anything, except to live his own life in the mountains. His bank transferred his child support every month right into my account, regardless of where he was working at the time, and he never got behind. He took Erika for his two weeks during the summer and the occasional ski weekend, and remembered her birthday with funny cards and sent her a gift card every Christmas. It wasn't thoughtful, but it worked. She never asked where her daddy was, never threatened to go live with him. She never asked why we split up, but it was all so uncomplicated that I would have told her.

I'd let the college talk go. That was my mistake. I'd printed the MCC application, the financial aid form with all of its fill-in bubbles. Scholarship applications. Early admission discounts. The whole works, but I left it all in a file folder on the counter.

I was a bit surprised, though, when the big manila envelope with the University of Montana logo came, and she whooped and texted rapid-fire to her friends.

"What's this about UM?" I asked her at dinner. She was picking at her salad as usual and drinking water with chunks of lemon.

"Don't freak out, Mom. God." She got up from the table and dumped her salad into the garbage.

"I'm not freaking out."

"Dad said he'd help pay. So I applied, and I got in. End of story." She grabbed her backpack and closed the bedroom door behind her.

End of story.

She graduated high school, in a blue satin robe with her cowgirl boots underneath. Dan sat beside me in the humid gym. He still wore a long ponytail, but it was threaded with gray. I was wearing the navy blue skirt that I wear when the bank president comes to visit, and the waistband dug into my fleshy middle. I was moved to tears by the graduation speaker (sure I was the only one listening), at Erika giggling down there in her folding chair with her friends, at Dan and I, how old we'd become.

We took her to lunch, steak and onion sandwiches and giant seasoned French fries with ranch for dipping, and Dan gave her a sip of his cold beer. Small talk, her feet tapping under the table, her phone whistling with every incoming text, until Dan paid the tab, she went off in a pickup truck with her girlfriends, free at last. Dan and I hugged, and he got into his silver Taurus (a rental, he told me, not that I asked) and drove west. He checked out of the Holiday Inn before the graduation, complained a bit about the coffee and the bed, glad he wasn't staying another night. He'd missed the senior ceremony at church the night before, the pictures with Father Anthony and the special communion. We hadn't talked like I wanted, to ask about his readiness to help her pay for four full years at UM. We didn't share any memories of her as a toddler or a tween, or of his plans during their upcoming two weeks together.

Summer passed—long days, short weekends. She worked at the coffee shop for $10.25 an hour plus a few meager tips (more than I made my first ten years at the bank), and I knew she saved well from going over her bank statements. She smelled like roasted coffee beans. I worked too, remembering my first years at the bank when we were required to wear stockings and below-the-knee skirts, and the year we were first allowed to wear slacks, but still with stockings. Nylons. Now, as long as the shoes were closed-toe, my legs could breathe. One of the tellers even had a nose ring, although it was tiny, silver and understated. Erika brought me iced coffee even though her shift ended at ten p.m. and I had to be at the bank by 7:30 the following morning. She floated the Tongue River on inner tubes, camped in a musty tent at Woodruff Park and came home smelling like campfire and old beer, but I didn't say anything. Dan surprised her with a long weekend in Denver at the beginning of their time in July, a couple Rockies games and Six Flags. She texted me upon their return to Montana, the short flight from Denver to Kalispell, "misssss youuuuuu—go grizzzzzz" followed by a picture of her in a U of M Grizzlies tank top. I bought her XL twin sheets for her dorm, a small fridge, a shower caddie, and bought myself a U of M polo shirt to wear on casual Fridays at work (collared shirts still required). When the admissions rep at MCC called to follow up on our previous interest, I told her chirpy voice that we'd changed our mind and hung up on her speech about the value of community colleges and transfer credits.

She cried a lot the week before she left. The old nursery rhyme *Monday's child is fair of face, Tuesday's child is full of grace. Wednesday's child is full of woe* . . . (how I hated that rhyme when she was an infant—who wants woe for their beautiful baby?) played in my head. Woe was in great supply that week. It seemed there was a constant stream of laughter followed by acute sobbing from the groups of girls behind her bedroom door. Girls hugging all the time and saying "I love you" when they left the house, the same girls who used to come in pink party dresses, bearing Barbie dolls wrapped in cupcake-printed paper, suddenly (almost overnight, it felt) with eyes full of makeup and hair tinted all colors, a few with small tattoos. Pictures taken and posted on Instagram, many that involved beer cans stacked in pyramids, or girls kissing each other. I called her on it and she blocked me, and after I threatened to stab all four of the tires on her used Subaru and told her she'd have to take the Greyhound to Missoula (not my finest hour), she relented and I could again be involved in her life through the veil of social media. I found her crying in front of a picture collage one morning, the one with every school picture from kindergarten on up, crooked bangs and missing teeth and cheerleader skirts and eyeliner. "I'm just going to miss you so much, Mom," she sobbed into my shoulder. I had to change my shirt before leaving for the bank. I don't think she'd been to bed, and I saved my tears for the drive to work. Yes, there was plenty of woe.

We were doing a data merge at the bank the day she wanted to get on the road, so we said goodbye in the driveway, she in her tank top and shorts, me in my pressed slacks and summer-weight sweater set, each of us with a travel mug of coffee. Her old Subaru was loaded to the roof and had a brand-new UM parking pass affixed to the rear window. Her graduation tassel still hung from the rearview. We'd finished our crying the last two nights, cuddling up on the couch and watching the movies she enjoyed as a child, popcorn purchased from the theater and brought home, fingerprints staining the couch. Ironing clothes and packing totes, marking lists, offering to buy her a month's worth of groceries but relenting with a couple of store-brand gift cards with her promise to buy at least one bunch of bananas. A gas card, a secret iTunes gift card tucked into her purse when she wasn't looking. Checking her admissions folder to verify tuition payment ("Dad said he was just finishing the details. God, stop worrying."), course schedule, campus map, orientation times. A giant box of tampons. Her birth control pills and condoms in the box with her makeup (I triple-checked). The thing that brought me to my knees: the green stuffed mouse that played Für Elise from a music box hidden in its rump, the toy I bought when I first found out I was pregnant, green for a girl or a boy. It was sitting in the side pocket of a duffel bag and I was reminded of the thousands of nights I heard her wind the song over and over while falling asleep, how the song would start out at tempo and get slower and slower until it wound down and she'd start it again. How many nights Dan cursed Beethoven for the song that was constantly in his head—"I can hear that damn thing all the time!"—but I knew I would pull up an audio file on my phone when I missed her.

"Call me when you get there," I told her, but she texted me from Billings, Bozeman, Butte, and then finally that night, just two words ("I'm here!!" and a smiley face) when she arrived in Missoula. I poured a glass of wine in celebration and sat at the kitchen table with the dog on my feet. It was quiet then, and I said a prayer for her, for her roommate, for her professors, for myself as an empty-nester, for Dan, who'd already made plans to drive down for the first football game. I remembered the day I found out I was pregnant, the way I wrapped the home test in tissues and then in a gift bag for Dan. He cried when he saw it; we were so happy to start our family. And her baptism at the church, during the lily-filled Easter service just days after she was born, the way she didn't even cry when the priest poured the holy water on her bald head, just stared at him with those heavily-lashed eyes, so interested in the world already. I was exhausted all the time during her infanthood, exhausted from caring for a newborn while having returned to work after only four weeks of leave, even though she was still up three times a night and Dan slept through it all, rolling over into the warm spot I left when I got up to change and nurse her. I had dark circles under my eyes and my hair was in a bad perm because I assumed the wash-and-air-dry curls would be easier in the mornings. And the precocious toddler, into everything and babbling up a storm, the preschooler who asked, "But *why?*" to absolutely everything. Dan was spending more and more time hunting, fishing, even some snowshoeing, and already he was talking about how the high prairie was making him feel anxious without mountains to break up the view. And when she started kindergarten I still felt so exhausted by the permission slips and the reading logs and the sight words and the birthday parties and the CCD classes where I took her because Dan had long stopped attending Mass, along with my promotion to Lending Administrator at the bank, that when the other mothers asked me, "So when are you having another?" I just smiled and pretended like we were discussing it when in truth Dan had already had a vasectomy. We bought a puppy from the classifieds; Erika named him Dr. Seuss.

Her daily texts from Missoula slowed to weekly ones, maybe a biweekly phone call with music playing in the background. Her Instagram showed girls getting ready for parties with curling irons and false eyelashes, football games with grizzly paw print temporary tattoos on their faces. Good-looking boys, too, with spiked hair and beer cans or video game controllers in their hands. It looked like college. I joined a Wednesday evening prayer group at church hosted by a nun visiting from India, mostly attended by old ladies with bluish hair and handkerchiefs in their sleeves. I enjoyed the nun's perfect Queen's English as much as I enjoyed the messages of the passages each week. I even signed up at the gym across the street from the bank and spent thirty minutes each day after work pedaling nowhere and listening to audiobooks. I walked Seuss and picked up his poop. He slept on Erika's empty bed, on an old high school cheerleading t-shirt I spread out for him. I ordered doggy steps so he wouldn't have to jump up or down onto the bed, and then I repeatedly chastised myself for being such an empty-nester that I had bought doggy steps. My cubicle at the bank held her framed senior portrait.

Her texting dropped off a couple weeks before Thanksgiving, a few pictures of a stack of books and highlighted notes written in her loopy hand, along with frowny faces and one-word, ellipse-heavy messages like "Studying . . ." and "ugggghh......." I called her several nights a week and left messages on her voicemail: "Hey, it's Erika, I guess you can leave a message, but no guarantees I'll call you back!" The first message I left, I told her that she should change it to something a little more adult-sounding, especially if she was expecting a call from a professor or a job interviewer, since I had suggested she find something to contribute to her bank account. The next few times, I left a simple, "It's Mom, please call me. I miss you and I love you." But she'd just text back, time-stamped in the wee hours, a quick note about passing a bio test or "acing" an interview at the coffee shop near her dorm. I texted her funny pictures of Seuss, hand-lettered signs propped up on his sleeping belly saying, "Call me (woof)! I miss you (woof!)" to no response. I started checking her Instagram like a stalker, barely able to input one page of loan data into the computer at work before refreshing her feed. She wasn't in a lot of pictures, but moms can always relate to being the one behind the camera, not in front of it. The Cat-Griz game, lots of raised middle fingers toward a group of fans wearing blue and gold. Pictures of the scoreboard showing the Griz winning, the team's huddle holding up the big bronze trophy. Blurry, low light shots inside of a bar, five girls taking shots all at once from glasses attached to a ski. The few selfies she was in were always arm-length and blurry, or filtered to look vintage. She looked thin, eyes unfocused. Although it was totally against the bank's rules, and my own Mom rules, I pulled up her bank account information to see where she was spending money. Typical debit card expenditures, like Target and REI, the UM bookstore, Washington-Grizzly Stadium (game day hot dogs). Deposits from me, deposits from Dan (First Bank of Polson the clue to me that he'd moved again), direct to her since he wasn't obligated to pay child support any more. She didn't have any bills with her cell phone plan attached to mine. A lot of checks had posted, though. Fifty dollars, a hundred. Twenty. No rhyme or reason to the amounts, no pattern to the dates the checks posted. I pulled up the digital images of several checks, made out to Cash, saw they were all cashed at a convenience store, that, after a quick Google search on my phone, I determined to be a couple blocks from campus. No big deal. Cash is king, right?

But she just wouldn't call me back, and that worried me. I called Dan, but his phone didn't even ring before going right to voicemail; I left a message anyway. I think

Seuss could tell I was worried, because he paced around the kitchen, nails too long and clicking, and he started sleeping on the foot of my bed instead of hers. I was distracted at work and once spilled my coffee over a new loan application trying to get at my phone to check out her social media. The loan officer came over to my cubicle after hearing me swearing and suggested I go for a walk. Bank customers were deliberately not looking at me, interested in their receipts or rummaging in their purses. I exchanged my indoor flats for my snow boots and put on my coat and scarf. I walked across the street to the coffee shop but didn't go in. I read the sign taped to the front window, over and over, like I was actually interested in signing up for a co-ed dodge ball tournament. I took a few deep breaths of the cold air and returned to the bank without coffee. Why was I so suspicious?

She was due to spend Thanksgiving with her roommate—this much from an earlier text. The long weekend at the family ranch in Dillon, her roommate with an extended family and always one more seat at the table. I planned to roast a small chicken, figuring on a few lunches and dinners with leftovers. The bank was open the Friday following, and I turned down offers from coworkers to join their families, didn't sign up for any of the church's Thanks Be to God shifts at the soup kitchen. I would eat my chicken, drink a glass of wine, enjoy the pint of pumpkin gelato I had picked up on a whim, take Seuss for a walk around the block afterward. Several bank employees had requested the Friday off, so I had offered to cover the teller line and wanted to show up rested for a day on my feet. Dan hadn't returned any of my messages, but The Weather Channel had mentioned several feet of fresh snow at Big Mountain and I figured he was skiing. I missed a call from the Dean of Students; she'd left a voicemail with no information, just requesting a call back. It was nearing the end of the semester, the four-day Thanksgiving weekend the first break since the start of the year, and I didn't call her back on the assumption that she was in vacation mode, or she was after a donation. I erased the message without writing down the return number.

The doorbell rang at 9 a.m. on Thanksgiving morning. I was still in my robe, over flannel pajamas and wool socks to ward off the chill in the house. Seuss barked but remained curled up in the buffalo-plaid orthopedic dog bed I'd gifted him, along with a stuffed turkey toy, for the holiday. I muted the parade on the TV and answered.

I hadn't opened the screen, so the first image of her was covered as though in a gray mist; once I unlocked and flung it open after I had wrapped her in my arms in a crushing hug and she struggled to pull away, the look of being shrouded by mist clung to her like a smell. I held her at arms' length, so surprised and shocked at her appearance and full of love to see her on the porch.

"God, Mom, you're gonna crush me." Her voice was flat. I could see, now, that she hadn't washed her hair in days, and it was crispy at the ends, likely from the brassy blonde dye she'd used at some point. Her skin was broken out and sore-looking, inflamed. She smelled metallic and smoky, like the sidewalk of a bar after a rain shower. Her clothes were wrinkled and a dark stain bloomed on her jeans.

"What a surprise, honey! Come in, come in!" Seuss had joined us at the doorway; he jumped up on his old legs and licked her hands. I closed the doors behind us, and as I did, I noticed her old Subaru wasn't in the driveway or parked at the curb.

She pushed the dog away, hard. "Get off me." She shuddered. "He stinks like shit."

I laughed, but uneasily. She had never minded him before, and it wasn't like her to use language like that around me. I told him to go lay down and he did without hesitating, back to his turkey and his bed.

I settled back on the couch. She paced. "I thought you were spending Thanksgiving with Piper."

"Aren't you happy to see me?" She sat on the arm of the recliner, then up, then to the mirror on the wall, where she examined her face closely. She picked at a few spots and then sighed angrily before pacing again.

"Of course I am. I'm just surprised, is all." Something wasn't right, her showing up like this, unannounced after no real contact, early in the morning, no car. And the way she looked! The freshman fifteen went the other way for her; her sweatshirt hung from the points of her shoulders. "I'm making chicken tonight and there's plenty. I have to work tomorrow, but—"

She cut me off. "That's okay, Mom. I just came to get some stuff." She gestured toward her bedroom, but what stuff I couldn't imagine. She'd either taken it or packed it away in the basement.

"Get some stuff? Erika, you came all the way from Missoula! Stay awhile!" I laughed again but could tell by the way her eyes darted around the room that something was really not right. Her nervous energy made me feel like I needed to do something. The entire situation was strange, and then, call it mother's intuition or whatever you will, I knew. I wasn't so old or so young that I couldn't remember where I was, what I was doing, when I heard about Kurt Cobain (in my parents' basement, MTV turned on surreptitiously while I did my chemistry homework, covalent bonds). I read the newspaper about local busts, the online magazines for the latest celebrity overdose. We'd even had a session on it during the parenting millennials classes at the church, what to look for—your child's appearance, unreliable and questionable spending patterns. Behavior changes. Mood. Father even handed out business cards for the parish's intervention team, but I couldn't imagine calling them on Thanksgiving, away from their families and their volunteer obligations to cast their judgmental eyes on me and their passages of Scripture at this girl who's shown up, this new Erika, on my doorstep. Yet here she was, and here it was, in my face.

"Sit down, honey. I'll make you some breakfast. Want coffee?" I headed into the kitchen. "Although you must be sick of coffee with your job and all!"

"My job?" She paused her pacing. "Oh, at the coffee shop. Yeah, that didn't really work out." I poked my head around the kitchen doorway; she was scratching at a scab on the top of her hand. She didn't seem to realize it was bleeding.

"Honey, here. Let me get you a paper towel." I didn't know what to do, how to handle it. Why couldn't I remember the session down in the basement conference room at church, the Help Your Child on Drugs session, I once joked about sounding like it was trying to help your child *do* drugs, the one I was so sure I didn't need and so didn't take notes? The only thing I could remember about that session was Father's little gray business cards and the smell of stale coffee and bad breath down there in the basement. I needed to do something with my hands—make her pancakes like when she was a little girl, pour her a cup of coffee—what did she mean, the job didn't work out? How did she get here at nine in the morning when Missoula was at the very least a seven-hour drive? Where was her car? I wet a paper towel in the sink and brought it to her. She was licking the blood from her hand.

"Jesus. Erika, what the hell are you doing?" I knelt down and dabbed at her hand with the towel. Her hands were twitching as though electricity was leaking out, not blood.

"Honey? Please tell me what's happening," I said softly. Seuss was chewing on his turkey, and she stared at him as he worked the squeaker hidden inside the tail. Her pupils were huge with just a rim of blue iris around them. She

58

reminded me of something, this sick, sick version of her, but I couldn't put my finger on it.

Suddenly she jumped up, the paper towel sticking to the wound on her hand. I followed her into the kitchen and watched while she poured coffee. She swiped at her eyes with her sleeve.

"Erika?" She didn't look at me, just stared out the window over the sink. I had a flashback of myself holding her as an infant, staring out that window during the night, she and I reflected back, as I bounced her in my arms, trying to get her to sleep.

I got angry. I slammed my fist on the countertop. Seuss startled and woofed from his bed. "Damn it, Erika. You show up here unannounced. I haven't heard a thing from you for days. You look like hell. What is going on?" I needed to hear her say it. Just say what it is, and I'll help, I thought.

She turned to me. Tears left muddy mascara tracks down her cheeks. I stepped to her and wrapped her in my arms.

"Mom," she whispered into my neck.

With her still in my arms, I walked her to the bathroom. "Shower," I told her. I heard her lock the bathroom door and the water start. I left a clean pair of leggings and a sweatshirt of mine beside the door for her to wear instead of her dirty and smelly clothes. Looking back, the sound of the door lock echoes throughout the house, but it couldn't possibly have been any louder than usual. I made pancakes and tinted them pink with food coloring the way I did for her birthdays. I made a fresh pot of coffee and added a dash of cinnamon to the basket so the house smelled homey and the coffee would have a subtle spicy taste. I set the small table in the kitchen with cloth napkins. I stacked the pancakes on a platter and set out butter, warmed syrup in the microwave. I tossed a special dental biscuit to Seuss when he wandered in. Filled his water bowl from the tap. I did everything I could, and still the shower ran. The pancakes were getting cold, the coffee.

I knocked on the bathroom door. "Erika, breakfast!" I thought of her hair, her smell, and figured she was standing under the spray, using my expensive shampoo, my products for aging skin, my razor, enjoying the cleansing of so-hot-you-can-barely-stand-it water, a shower without flip flops and five other girls in stalls next to you, their hair clogging up the shared drains. I sat at the table, nibbled on a plain pancake, drank a cup of coffee. The cinnamon tasted sharp.

Seuss had finished his dental chew and I let him out the back door. I knocked again on the bathroom door. "Erika!" The water was still running. I knocked harder, using my fist instead of my knuckles. "Erika, time to get out!" No sound except the water. I paced the hallway, knocking each time I went by. I thought of her skin, the way it was so red, the way she picked at it. Her pupils. It clicked, what she reminded me of. The super-sized billboards all over the state. The ads on TV. Grim and borderline obscene, outlining your life on meth. It used to be the egg in the frying pan, now it was a dirty girl, a man's hand holding her down, a slogan about fifteen bucks for sex. Cracked lips over burned-out teeth. That wasn't Erika, oh but it was, wasn't it? The images of her cashed checks flashed, the address of the convenience store where they had been cashed, so close to her dorm. The amounts. Cheap, but meth was, wasn't it? That was the point, right? The call from the Dean that I'd ignored. Her bleeding skin and fried hair. Why did I let her go?

I was slow on the uptake, but not stupid. I pounded on the door now, both fists, kicked at it with my wool sock. I screamed her name, screamed and pounded, kicked and yelled. My voice raised into a shrill octave. Somewhere, Seuss whined. I cursed the solid oak door and frame of the old house, cursed the lock-from-the-inside mechanism. "Erika! Open the fucking door!" The shower ran and ran. It had to be ice cold by now, the water heater taxed. I grabbed a stool from the kitchen, stainless steel legs and barn wood seat, rustic, heavy. I banged it without thought against the glass doorknob, original to the house, the iron plate. The door knob shattered on the floor, the lock clattered to the ground.

I pushed my way in. The shower curtain was open, water splashing into the porcelain tub. She was dressed still, crumpled on the floor by the toilet like a dirty rug. So small.

I screamed. I flailed at her, gathered her into my arms on the floor; I was moving as though underwater, heavy, slow. Her head lolled back and I could see the whites of her eyes under her half-shut lids. "Erika! Baby, wake up! Erika!" I laid her gently back on the floor—phone, phone, phone, call someone—covered her with a towel— "Baby, I'll be right back. I'll be right back"—I chanted to her as I ran into the kitchen for the phone—Seuss barking, barking, jumping, jumping at the back door, paws scraping on the wood—I could barely hear the dispatcher or my own voice as I screamed into the receiver—the phone on the seat of the toilet and held her, held her, held her, stroked her hair, and kissed her face.

I didn't turn off the shower. One of the EMTs must have, once they arrived to load her up on the stretcher, after a needle clattered to the floor and blood spurted from her arm on the floor on the wall drip, drip, drip, a tight yellow strap binding her down, bagged oxygen pump, pump, pump by hand into her face. The siren from the ambulance, the lights, brought the neighbors in their pajamas and day-off clothes to their porches, and I noticed, strange the things you notice, as one of the EMTs helped me into my jacket and my winter boots and then into the ambulance, the smell of wood stove in the outside air, and that Jack Sondberg from next door had Seuss by the collar. The wet pink shine of all of the open mouths.

Those wet mouths asked questions I wouldn't—couldn't—answer. The EMTs didn't look at each other, didn't pass knowing glances to each other over her body. I heard them say IV user, I heard them say precautions, Hep, HIV. OD and naloxone, we need more naloxone! The nurse at the hospital called and called Dan's cell phone until finally leaving a message at the ski patrol office. They made me wait in a place marked "Consultation," but it was just a regular hospital room without a bed. Easy-clean floor, green vomit bags coiled on the counter like snakes. There was a cord attached to a red switch plate that was stickered "Pull for Emergency." I thought about pulling it, pulling it so hard it broke off in my hand. Father Anthony showed up—who called him?—and he was in a Dallas Cowboys jersey over his collar and was apologetic about it. He had the nun with him, the one from my prayer group, her dark Indian skin showing every wrinkle in the overhead fluorescent lights. They held my hands, prayed at me. The PA, with his grave face, saying crisis or critical, or maybe it was 'copter, because he soon led me out to the painted X in the back parking lot where they had Erika on another stretcher and were putting us inside the helicopter, handing me a set of headphones, and I knew she was alive still but they wouldn't let me hold her hand. She had wires and patches snaking all over and tubes in her arm, oxygen mask over her face. They'd stripped her clothing, she was covered, barely, in a blue flowered gown, and I could see the way her collarbone strained at her skin, ribs laddering her chest. The sores on her skin crusty and red. Her dirty hair and a vein in her neck so blue and full of her blood—alive!—I wanted to scream. I couldn't hear anything even through the headphones, but as we lifted off toward Billings, I could see a few, or maybe a million, columns of smoke from chimneys.

I thought of her, the way I used to comb out the tangles in her hair before school, how she'd squirm and squeal if I pulled too hard. Her fourth birthday, when I took her to a salon and surprised her with an ear piercing. The day she learned to ride a bike; the whole week she dressed Seuss up in doll clothes and walked him around and around the yard on a leash. Her first period, the morning before a junior high basketball game and her fear about the white shorts the team wore. The first days of school, the call-in-sick days when she had a fever, the proms, the dates, movies and friends and boys and everything I worked so hard for, keeping her here instead of agreeing to stay with Dan and live his life in the mountains, when our lives were so clearly right here so she could join her friends in high school. The agreement, how easily I was persuaded, to send her off to Missoula. To what? It wouldn't have happened here, I told myself as the helicopter climbed and bounced in the air. Right? It wouldn't have happened if she'd just listened to me, just stayed right here, with me and the dog. And I thought of the billboard she reminded me of, how it loomed right off the interstate and greeted everyone with its sick picture, right here as though advertising our very own town, and I looked out the small window and saw the frost that covered the cottonwoods along the river, saw the chimney smoke of all the families having a warm fire on this Thanksgiving day and we were in this helicopter, and the crew was poking and testing and documenting and doing all of their things to keep her alive, and I thought, Burn it down. Burn the whole damn thing.

About the Author

Sarah Rau Peterson is a first-generation Montanan. She lives with her husband and two children near Miles City, where she divides her time between the family's cattle ranch, her middle school history classroom, and her children's activities. She publishes occasionally in *The Montana Quarterly*.

About the Press

Unsolicited Press is a small publishing house in Portland, Oregon and is dedicated to producing works of fiction, poetry, and nonfiction from a range of voices, but especially the underserved. Our team has published books that aren't afraid to take on topics of race, gender, identity, feminism, patriarchy, mental health, and more. The team is comprised of hardworking volunteers that are passionate about literature.

Learn more at www.unsolicitedpress.com.

CPSIA information can be obtained
at www.ICGtesting.com
Printed in the USA
LVHW101944260422
717290LV00007B/297